First American edition, 1986
Text copyright © Anita Harper, 1986
Illustrations copyright © Susan Hellard, 1986
All rights reserved. Published simultaneously in Canada by General Publishing Co. Limited,
Toronto.
Originated and published in Great Britain by Piccadilly Press, 1986.
Printed in Hong Kong
L.C. number: 86-4950
G. P. Putnam's Sons, 51 Madison Avenue, New York, New York 10010

ISBN 0-399-21365-1
First impression

IT'S NOT FAIR!

by Anita Harper

illustrated by Susan Hellard

G. P. Putnam's Sons · New York

When they brought
my baby brother home,
everyone fussed over him.

It wasn't fair.

"What about me?"
"You're a big girl now,"
my mother said.

I'm not THAT big.

People are always doing things for him.
I have to do things for myself.

It's not fair!

If he makes a mess, it's all right.

If I make a mess, I get into trouble.

That's not fair!

When we go out, I have to walk.
But my baby brother can ride.

It makes me mad.

When the baby-sitter is here, and my brother screams, she tries to find out what's wrong.

When I scream,
she tells me to be quiet.

It's not fair!

Now my brother's getting bigger.
The other day, we went for a walk in the rain.
He wanted to walk,
but my mother wouldn't let him.

He didn't think
that was fair.

And when we go to the park,
he wants to slide down the hill,
but he isn't big enough.

He doesn't think
that's fair either!

When I go to playgroup,
my brother wants to go too,
but he can't.

He doesn't think that's fair at all.

Now, when my friends come over, my brother wants to play with us, but he's too small.

He lets us know
he doesn't
think that's fair.

Sometimes I'm allowed to stay up late,
but my brother has to go to bed.
He screams and screams,

because it's not fair.

My brother has started to talk now.
Today I'm going to a party and he can't go.
Do you know what he said?

"It's not fair!"